'I mustn't forget the pictures, you see. They are all I've got left. Not that they're much use,' he added mournfully. 'It's like trying to do a jigsaw puzzle with bits that don't fit.'

'I'm good at jigsaws. I'll help you. Tell me what they are.'

Grey began to chant:

'Girl on a rocking-horse
Saddle of red
That old green door
Chimney-pots
One two
Three four
A golden key
And last of all
Six stone steps to . . .'

He left off. To where? If only he knew.

Sounds more like a riddle,' Mark said.

'Jigsaw . . .? Riddle . . .? What's the difference if you can't work it out?' Grey said sadly.

The Rainbow Sandwich

MARJORIE DARKE
Illustrated by Joanna Worth

MAMMOTH

First published in Great Britain 1989
by Methuen Children's Books Ltd
Published 1990 by Mammoth
an imprint of Mandarin Paperbacks
Michelin House, 81 Fulham Road, London SW3 6RB

Mandarin is an imprint of the Octopus Publishing Group

Text copyright © 1989 Marjorie Darke
Illustrations copyright © 1989 Joanna Worth

ISBN 0 7497 0310 5

A CIP catalogue record for this title
is available from the British Library

Printed in Great Britain
by Cox and Wyman Ltd, Reading, Berkshire

Contents

1   Lost and Found   *page* 7
2   Grey and the Rocking-horse   *page* 15
    Friend
3   Flying Tricks and Flowerpots   *page* 28
4   A Key for Dressing Up   *page* 44
5   The Green Door   *page* 61
6   A Game of Cricket   *page* 77
7   Stone Steps and Sandwiches   *page* 87

1
Lost and Found

'Mind out!' yelled the crane driver.

The men throwing slates from the roof, scrambled down their ladders and stood out of the way. A big iron ball, hanging from the crane, swung back then forwards and . . . THUMP! The wall shuddered. Back went the ball. Forward again and . . . CRRRUNCH! Bricks, plaster, slates, wood, fell in a great cloud of dust that rose up around the tottering chimney-pots.

Down below in the cellar, the little ghost jerked awake. He was lying in his favourite bed, an old trunk full of comfortable newspaper, dreaming about his friend, Albert, when the terrible noise came again.

CRRRRUNCHCHCH   CRRRRACK!
Walls groaned. Stone floor shook.

'Holy spooks!' He clapped his long thin hands over his pointed ears and shot through the trunk lid. His cobwebby hair was stiff with fright. 'Here . . . what's going on?'

Nobody answered, but a big chunk of ceiling plaster fell straight through him, making his bones rattle. Ghost-pimples stood out all over his skinny body.

The terrible noise crashed and rumbled on over his head. It must be thunder. How he hated thunderstorms!

CCCCRRRRACK GGGRRROWL BANG CRRRRUMP!

Never in all his born nights had he known a storm like this. Dust filled his mouth and made him cough. He was sneezing with dust, crying with dust — bits of plaster falling around and through him so fast he didn't know whether he was coming or going.

And then the whole lot caved in.

'Thunderbolts!' he shrieked, and dived straight through the cellar wall into the earth.

He came up next to an enormous dirty-yellow monster, whose tremendously long neck was too thin to hold up its big round head. It was guarding a great pile of rubbish. The ghost stared. Where was his old haunting-place?

The monster growled. Its terrible head swung towards the ghost, scaring him so badly he took off. Forgetting all about gliding like a proper spook, he tripped over his nightshirt, fell into a tree, tangled with a fence and went headlong into a duck pond. His poor bones shook and rattled until they almost fell apart.

'And it's my sleep-time. I should be abed!' He was almost in tears. 'Any ghost worth a groat is snoring this time of day,' and catching his toe in a hole, down he went.

The hole was in a bank. It looked dark and inviting. The little ghost crawled inside, hoping to find somewhere to sleep. But the place was seething with rabbits! They nibbled at his nightshirt, and kept hopping through him, making sleep impossible.

The next day he settled in a tree trunk – but the birds and leaves were so noisy he didn't get a wink of sleep there either.

After that he tried all sorts of places – buckets, cowsheds, haystacks, gateposts, a couple of

9

carts, several hedges. Not one was comfortable. He even stretched out under a paving slab, but the worms wriggled and tickled so much he couldn't get to sleep for laughing.

Days and nights got mixed up. Weeks went by; months. . . . The little ghost couldn't remember how long he had been travelling. Where he had come from, where he meant to go, was a mystery. Even his name slipped away with the passing years.

'I'm lost!' He spread out his tattered night-shirt and gazed down at his battered feet. 'Look at me! Thin as a pin and full of holes. If I go on like this I shan't be here at all.'

By mistake he had drifted into a town. How he hated towns! But he was too tired and upset to travel any further. Rattling down into a gutter, he fell fast asleep.

'Mind out!' yelled the car driver, blaring his horn and making his brakes squeal.

The little ghost was sitting up before his popping eyes were open, just as a man on a bike swerved straight through him.

'Holy spooks!' The ghost leapt up and back,

but not in time to miss the water. A bus splashed through a puddle as it halted by the kerb.

People began to get down from the bus. They took no notice of the ghost propped up against the bus-stop. They barged through him, stepped on his toes, put their elbows in his ears – shoving and spinning him like a roundabout until he was dizzy.

The last two people got off together. A woman in a red macintosh with a small boy wearing an anorak and wellingtons. The

woman walked straight through the little ghost as if he wasn't there, but the boy stopped. He and the ghost stared at each other.

'Come along, Mark. We don't want to be late for Gran.'

Mark didn't move. 'How long is she staying?'

'Until she finds her new house. . . . I told you that already.' The woman took his hand.

'Sort of coming home, isn't it?' the boy said, keeping an eye on the ghost. 'Back where she lived when she was a girl.'

'That's right. And at this rate, she'll probably be home before us – making tea. Do come on!' She tugged his hand.

Here we go, thought the ghost. Through me as usual!

The boy stepped carefully out of the way, and as he passed the ghost he put out his free hand and touched him. His fingers were warm and the little ghost shivered. The boy shivered too, as his hand slid slowly through the tattered nightshirt. Then he smiled. A very big, very pleased smile.

'Mark!' The woman gave another tug. 'What's got into you?'

'I got into him you mean,' Mark said. 'Didn't you see the ghost, Mum?'

The little ghost felt cold with delight. This was the nicest thing that had happened since, since . . . since he couldn't remember when. He was so excited, his cobwebby hair began to crackle and spark. He trotted after his new friend, determined to go along with him for the present. This was better than being lost. Growing bolder he crept up beside Mark. Then he waved. At the last minute remembering to glide and show he knew how to behave like a proper spook as they moved along the pavement together.

2
Grey and the Rocking – horse Friend

The noisy town was being left behind. Shops, garages, a church, a school – now quiet houses lined the road. The little ghost smiled at Mark.

'Can't you *see* that ghost, Mum?' Mark pointed at him. 'You must! He is there. See-through like a dirty window. Everything is misty on the other side.'

'*Me* . . . a dirty window?' The little ghost was shocked.

'He talks! Mum, he can talk!'

'Of course I can talk. You talk. Why shouldn't I?'

'Mum, he answered me.'

'Yes, dear.' Mum went on walking.

Mark frowned. 'You don't believe me.'

'It isn't that I don't believe you, dear. We just haven't time for nonsense now.'

'It's not nonsense. It's true!'

The ghost shook his cobwebby head until it looked like a swirling mop. 'You're wasting your time,' he said. 'Grown-up folk are deaf and blind when it comes to us ghosts. I know. I've been doing my best to haunt them for years. They don't take any notice.'

'What's haunt?' Mark asked.

'Oh, I hide, then pop out through a door or wall, or through anything that happens to be there at the time – but it has to be when people aren't expecting me.'

'Sort of hide-and-seek?'

'You could call it that. I'm supposed to scare them.' The ghost sighed. 'The trouble is it doesn't work. I mean, how can you scare somebody if they don't see you? It's not that I haven't tried. I have. Everything I can think of – I pull terrible faces, yell, rattle my bones. Useless!'

'Rattle them now,' Mark said.

The ghost was surprised, but obligingly started at the top of his bony head and shook himself all the way down to the ends of his long thin fingers and last blisters on his pale skinny toes. His bones clicked and plopped.

'Rain's starting again,' Mum said. 'Listen to it! Hurry up, we don't want to get wet.'

'See what I mean?' the ghost said. 'She thinks I'm the patter of rain.'

'Well I know it's you rattling, and I can see you.'

'Are you scared?' asked the ghost hopefully.

'No.'

'Oh.' It was very disappointing, but the ghost couldn't let this chance slip past without another try. Putting his fingers into his mouth he stretched and stretched, then stuck out his thin green tongue. Opening his eyes very wide he let out a long howl: 'YAAAAHHHH!' Straightening himself, he glanced at Mark. 'How about that?'

Mark was shivering. 'Great! Do it again!'

'YAAAAHHHH EEEEEEEK BOOOOOO!' shrieked the ghost joyfully, gliding uphill and flapping his arms. He was sure everything was going to be all right now. There would be quiet fields on the other side of this hill. Already his bones were beginning to feel at home.

He reached the top. And stopped. Crawling down the other side were nothing but rows and rows of houses standing in shadowy garden patches. Street lamps switched on suddenly, throwing strips of orange light across hard pavement and parked cars.

'Another town!' the little ghost was horrified.

Mark had caught up with him. 'That's not a town, that's our estate. See the big tree over there? I live in the house next to it. With the red door.'

'Why isn't it green?' It ought to be green.'

'Because Dad painted it red. You are funny!'

The ghost didn't feel at all funny. He felt very strange. Pictures kept pushing into his mind.

'I suppose you've got to go home now,' Mark was saying. 'Where do you live?'

'Here and there.' The ghost waved his hand vaguely. His bones felt out of joint like the pictures in his head. Nothing fitted.

'But where specially?' Mark insisted.

'Can't remember,' said the ghost, sulkily.

'What's your name then?'

'Can't remember. You do ask a lot of questions.'

'Can't you remember *anything*?'

The ghost shook down his bones in a huff. 'Of course I can. That green door for one thing. Then there was a . . .' he was going to say 'rocking-horse', but they had reached Mark's house and a tall woman in jeans and pink spectacles was smiling in the open doorway.

'There you are at last,' she interrupted, and a small brown and white dog hurtled past her, barking and jumping up at Mark. 'Plum *is* pleased to see you. So am I.'

Plum seemed pleased to see the little ghost as well. She sniffed round his long pale feet, wagging her tail. Then bounced a welcome, putting up her paws but falling through him. Not minding, and bouncing all over again.

Gran was laughing. 'Look at that dog! She's gone quite daft. Come on in – that's right. I let myself in and put the kettle on ready for you. We'll have a nice cup of tea in no time.'

'Wait, Gran!' Mark cried, as she began to close the door. 'Grey's not in. Come and have some tea, Grey.'

The ghost looked round for Grey. The cat sitting on the window-sill cleaning its paws, was ginger-coloured. There was nobody else. He hung back, suddenly shy. 'If you mean me, I only drink mist-shakes. And you don't have to bother about shutting me out.'

Mum laughed. 'You and your invisible friends!' She ruffled Mark's hair. 'Chatter chatter all the way home. You should have heard him, Gran.' She shut the door.

The little ghost sat down on the garden wall and tried out his new name. 'Grey Greeaay Grrrrey GRRRRAAAAEEEE!' Yes, it had possibilities. But he wasn't so sure that this was the right kind of house to haunt. It was new and small. Not what he had been used to.

But what had he been used to?

For a long time he sat, trying to remember. The sky grew dark and the cat jumped down and came to rub around his legs, purring. He had almost decided to give up and move on when sudden light streamed down from an upstairs window. Startled, he glanced up. His hair began to crackle with excitement. On the other side of the window was the head of an old *rocking-horse*.

Curtains swished across. Light and horse disappeared.

In seconds, Grey had gone through the red front door, up the stairs, passing through Mum on the way, and into the wall on the other side of the landing with such a rush that he lost his balance and arrived on all fours.

There was a shout of laugher. Light from the landing showed Mark sitting up in bed.

Grey pulled the rest of himself through the wall and staggered to his feet. He rubbed his bruised knee-bones. 'I wouldn't laugh if you fell down,' he said crossly.

Mark tried to stop, but little snorts kept breaking out. 'Can't help it. You did look funny! Are you . . . all right?'

Grey tested bits of himself. 'I think so.'

'Why didn't you come through the door? It's open.'

Grey was combing out the tangles in his hair with his fingers. 'Who needs doors?' he said loftily.

'I do. Mostly.' Mark tumbled out of bed and shot on to the landing. As he went past, Grey realised what he meant to do.

'Wait . . . WAIT!' he bawled, tottering

back through the wall and meeting Mark nose to nose as he skidded up against the wallpaper. 'Wraiths and Shapes! Do you want to knock yourself out?'

'You didn't,' Mark said.

'It's different for me.'

'Why?'

'Part of my job, that's why. I told you what I have to do. Walk through walls. Bone rattling. A bit of flying when called for.'

Mark's eyes shone. 'Will you take me flying?'

'I might,' Grey said cautiously. 'It all depends. Crash landings can be painful.'

'But if we held hands you'd keep me safe. Or you could give me a piggyback,' Mark said eagerly. 'Let's try now. Let's try going through the wall first. Then we can fly after.' He tried to grasp Grey's hand, but slipped through. 'You're cold.'

'It is a bit nippy,' Grey agreed.

Mark looked him over. 'Your nightie's too thin. You need a jumper and some jeans and socks and an anorak and . . .'

'You talk too much!' Grey took Mark's hand and this time held fast. 'I'll go through first. Sideways. I'll pull you after me. Ready?'

Mark nodded, but there was no time. Foot-steps sounded on the stairs.

'Out of bed, Mark?' Dad picked him up.

'Grey and me were just going through the wall,' Mark told him.

Dad laughed. 'You've been dreaming. You are still half asleep.' He tucked him back into bed. 'No more sleep-walking,' Dad said, and went out, closing the door.

'Grey,' Mark whispered. 'Are you there?'

'Yes.' Grey glided to the rocking-horse and climbed into the new yellow saddle.

Mark yawned. 'You don't mind me calling you Grey, do you? You are sort of grey.'

'I don't mind.' Grey began to rock and hum quietly to himself.

'Grey,' Mark said again.

'What?'

'Don't go away, will you? We can go through the wall in the morning, and fly, and . . . what are you singing?'

'Pictures.'

'You can't sing pictures.'

'I can. I mustn't forget them, you see. They are all I've got left. Not that they're much

use,' he added mournfully. 'It's like trying to do a jigsaw puzzle with bits that don't fit.'

'I'm good at jigsaws. I'll help you. Tell me what they are.' Mark yawned again.

Grey began to chant:

> 'Girl on a rocking-horse
> Saddle of red
> That old green door
> Chimney-pots
> One two
> Three four
> A golden key
> And last of all
> Six stone steps to . . .'

He left off. To where? If only he knew. The rocking-horse slowed down.

'Sounds more like a riddle,' Mark said.

'Jigsaw . . .? Riddle . . .? What's the difference if you can't work it out?' Grey said sadly.

Mark blinked sleepily. 'We could try together. Gran says two heads are better than one.' He settled down in his bed. 'Cherry'll help. That's three heads.'

'Who is Cherry?'

'She lives next door. She's good at finding

things. She found Sam when he got lost.'

'Who is Sam?'

'Our cat. You saw him on the window-sill.'
Mark's eyelids drooped. 'In th'morning,' he
mumbled. 'Start looking . . . then.'

'Hold on,' Grey said – then heard a little
snore. He wanted to say that morning was his
bed-time. But Mark was asleep.

Grey patted the dappled neck of the horse,
which seemed strangely familiar. He rocked
again. Backwards. Forwards. Harder. Quicker.
An idea dropped into his bony head and
opened up like a flower.

No need for rules about my bed-time,' he told
the horse. 'Sleep now and get up with Mark,
that's what I'll do. That way I can keep an eye
on him. We'll do things together.' He smiled.
Together sounded like a friend. There had
been another friend once, hadn't there? For a
moment he felt sad again. Then giving his
bones a shake, he yawned and stretched. Mark
was his friend now.

He looked round for somewhere to sleep.

Bed? No – too full of boy.

Chair? No – too hard.

He spotted the chest of drawers. That was

more promising. Lots of soft things lived in drawers. He slid off the rocking-horse, giving it a final pat, and did his super-trick. Hovering on his back, mid-air, level with the drawer, he slid in sideways and made a perfect landing on top of Mark's pants. Finding a pair of socks, he tucked them comfortably under his head and pulled a jumper up to his chin.

'We're all right now, bones,' he said, and closed his eyes.

3
Flying Tricks
and Flowerpots

There were little people moving about inside a box on the kitchen shelf. They had loud voices. As loud as real people. They were shouting as they walked through a field.

Grey couldn't understand it at all. He perched on the draining-board, legs dangling, and stared.

Just then the door opened and in trotted Plum. She made a dive at Grey's feet and tried to lick them, wagging herself from tail to nose.

'She likes you.' Mark was hopping about, mug of milk in one hand, toast in the other.

'Does she?' Grey was pleased. There was a clothes peg sitting on top of the box of people. He took a breath and blew at it. Away flew the peg, hitting Gran on the shoulder as she came into the kitchen.

'Careful, Mark!' She juggled with the cup and saucer she was carrying. 'Stick throwing is for outside.'

'Wasn't me.' Mark went on hopping. 'Grey threw it.'

'Grey?'

'That ghost.'

Mum and Gran exchanged looks.

'Ghost or no ghost,' Gran said, 'I don't want tea down my front when I'm about to go house hunting. I want to look tidy when I call on Mr Cox this morning.'

'For goodness' sake, sit down, Mark,' Mum said. 'You'll give yourself hiccups eating on the move like that.'

Mark stuffed the last of the toast into his mouth and hopped over to the box. He turned a knob and the people in the field disappeared. There was a blare of sound as if a pile of tin cans had been kicked over, then – thud thud thud thud thud . . .

Plum howled.

Ghost-pimples came out all over Grey. His eyes popped. His cobwebby hair stood on end.

The box was full of different people now. They had glittering clothes and hair of blue and green, and they were waving their arms. Singing. The din was tremendous, but the people remained curiously small.

Sliding off the draining-board, Grey went to the box and peered closely at it. He touched the people. They were warm and flat. It was very strange. He began to tremble.

'Must you have the telly on so loud?' Mum asked. She glanced up from the loaf she was cutting. 'What's happened to that screen? It's gone all misty.'

'Everything goes misty when you look through Grey. He's leaning on it,' Mark explained. 'And I want it loud.'

'Weather conditions more like.' Mum put down the bread knife, and went to the television. 'And *I* want it quieter.'

Grey whisked round the back of the box to see what the little dancers looked like from behind, but they had vanished. All he could see was a dark bulge, as if the box had grown a hump.

'Mu . .um!' Mark complained, spitting crumbs. He went back to turn up the sound.

'NO!' Mum said, very loud.

Mark stumped to the draining-board, dumped his mug and went out of the back door, slamming it. Plum howled again.

Grey sighed. This morning was turning out all wrong. He thought of nipping into the box to join the dancers as they seemed to be enjoying themselves. He put a cautious hand inside to test before all of him slid in, and drew it out again fast. It was baking in there! How could they stand such heat? Drifting back to the sink, he slid through into the garden.

Mark was moodily booting a plastic flowerpot down the path. 'It's not fair,' he said, seeing Grey. 'First I go and bang my nose trying to follow you through my bedroom wall, now Mum won't let me have the telly on loud enough.'

'What's telly?' Grey asked.

'You don't *know*?' Mark stared.

'Would I ask if I did? What is it?'

Mark considered. 'A sort of box that has moving pictures. You saw it in the kitchen.'

'But those people living inside were much too small!'

Mark began to laugh. 'You are silly. They

aren't really small . . . and they don't live in the telly, they're miles away. A camera was filming them.'

Grey opened his mouth to ask what a camera was, and closed it again. He was feeling dizzy. Being awake at this time of day took some getting used to – he wasn't sharp enough to tackle more new things.

'Didn't you have a telly in your old home place?' Mark asked.

'Can't remember,' Grey said shortly. His bones drooped.

'Never mind.' Mark felt sorry for him. 'You can watch ours now.' He dribbled the flowerpot further along the path, and with a hard side kick sent it spinning into the cabbages where Sam, the ginger cat, was having a lick down of his fur. Sam sprang up and through Grey, landing on top of the fence – back arched; fur spiked.

'Wraiths and Shapes!' Grey shook out his ruffled bones. 'What d'you take me for – a letter-box?' He stalked to the larch-board fence, in half a mind to keep going. He was almost through when he felt Mark trying to take hold of his hand.

'I want to go with you . . . please! A fence is thinner than a wall. Don't go away, Grey!'

Grey slowed down.

'*Please*, Grey?'

'Oh very well!' Grey gripped Mark's hand tightly and began to pull. Smooth as silk his own arm came back to him without so much as a crease in his nightshirt. He was pleased. This was more like it! Elbow. Wrist . . .

'Ow!' Mark said.

Grey tugged.

'Ow! I'm stuck.'

Grey let go, and because he didn't really want to go away, did a neat cartwheel back into Mark's garden.

Mark was rubbing his knuckles. 'I've got an idea. We won't bother going through, we'll fly over instead. You did promise to show me how.'

'I did no such thing!' Grey said, taken aback.

'Yes you did. When we talked about flying last night.'

'I said I might. Besides, it isn't that easy.'

'You mean you don't know how to fly.'

'I mean it isn't that easy for *you*. Of course

33

I can fly,' he began to boast: 'Didn't I win a gold star for the best aerial spook display of the year? I've got a certificate to prove it,' adding rashly: 'I was very good at nose dives, and rolls, and figures of eight. I even looped the loop!'

'You are remembering!' Mark said excitedly. 'Show me!'

'What, now?' Grey was startled. The truth was he couldn't remember in his head doing any of these tricks. It was more of a strong feeling inside his bones.

'Yes, now,' Mark demanded.

Grey shut his eyes. Little shivers of alarm rattled his bones. He tried to remember how to set about flying, and couldn't. Think, he told himself, THINK! To calm his bones he took an enormous breath puffing out his nightshirt, and something strange began to happen. He had to open his eyes to make sure, and found his feet on a level with Mark's nose. The ground had moved away!

'WHEEEE! I'm airborne! Look at me – I'm doing it! Now d'you believe me?'

'That's not proper flying,' Mark said. 'Move about.'

Obligingly, Grey began to move around the garden like a hovercraft. He sailed over the cabbages as if they were waves on the sea. Zoomed over a blackcurrant bush, and finished with a couple of airhops over watering-can and bucket.

'I suppose that's a bit better,' Mark said.

'A bit? *A BIT!*' Grey was so indignant he didn't take any notice of the scrabbling noises on the other side of the fence. 'It takes a lot of skill and practice to float around without bumping into things.'

The scrabbling noises were getting louder. A voice called: 'Who are you talking to, Mark?' Curly brown hair and dark eyes appeared above the fence. Then a grin. A girl in a bright yellow sweater, jeans and red boots, settled beside Sam. She gazed at Grey. 'Mark, you've got a ghost in your garden.'

Grey cheered up. 'You must be Cherry.' He knew at once that he was going to like her. 'Grey is the name,' bowing deeply. 'I'm haunting Mark's house for the time being.'

Cherry's eyes rounded. 'Mark, he can talk!'

'I know that . . . and he flies. He's going to give me a lesson.'

'And me!' Cherry stood up unsteadily. 'Is this the way?' Spreading her arms she flapped as if she had wings.

'NOT LIKE THAT!' Grey yelled as her boots slipped. He saw her topple sideways, and in the nick of time crouched and blew upwards with every scrap of ghost-breath he could muster. She went through him, floating feather-light on to the path. Grey shivered. First a cat posts itself through me, now a girl, he thought. It's getting to be a habit.

Cherry scrambled to her feet. 'I flew I flew. It's easy.' She made for the fence and was half-way to the top, fingers and boots digging into the wood, before Grey had picked himself up.

'Wait!' he warned, as she wobbled upright. 'You can't manage by yourself.'

She didn't listen. She jumped.

So did Sam.

Grey managed to draw in enough air to pump out another cushion of ghost-breath and prevent a crash landing, but had no time to aim straight. Cherry and Sam went sideways into the cabbages. Sam took off again as soon as he hit the earth, vanishing behind the dustbin.

Mark, who had been watching with his mouth open, suddenly dashed over and picked up the bucket. Turning it upside down against the fence, he boosted himself up. He raised his hands above his head as if he was standing on the side of a swimming bath.

Horrified, Grey gulped in more air, shooting it out in one tremendous burst. At the same moment a gust of wind caught Mark as he dived. The two currents of air met and sent him sailing up towards the roof, throwing him against the chimney and the TV aerial. He slid on to the slates and lay staring up at puffy white clouds in a sky of deep blue. At first he was too scared to move. Then growing bolder, he sat up carefully.

The garden looked far away. He had a funny sinking feeling as he looked down at Sam hiding by the garage, then down at Cherry twisting round to see the dirt on the seat of her jeans. The sinking feeling grew worse. He shut his eyes. When he tried opening them a crack Grey was rising like a helicopter, travelling sideways. He landed close to Mark on the slates.

'Some people are always in too much of a

rush,' Grey said with a twitch of his bones. 'Some people have cloth ears and don't obey instructions. Some people like to . . .' He glanced at Mark. 'Are you listening?'

'Yes.' But Mark was much more interested in what he could see across the roof-tops. Everything looked so different from up here. He felt safe with Grey, and wanted to tell him about all the interesting things. 'Grey, look – our milkman's got a new poster on his van. DRINKA PINTA! D'you like milk, Grey?' He didn't wait for an answer: 'Somebody's put a pony in that field with the pond. I never knew there was an old bike behind the bungalow shed, nor about that gnome . . . four gnomes I mean. See them, Grey? Under those big flowerpots! Oh look . . .' he began to giggle. 'Mrs Dilkes's bag's bust. All her apples are rolling about the pavement. Hey, there's Gran taking Plum for a walk. Gran . . . Gran . . .' he tried to stand up and wave, but Grey pressed him down.

'Do you want to fall and hurt yourself?'

'I wouldn't. Didn't you see how I flew up here? I can fly down just the same.'

'Blew up here,' Grey corrected. 'There are

one or two things we must get straight before you try any more wild flights.'

'What sort of things?'

'For a start, you can't fly without help from me. So don't go diving off this roof.'

'How will I get down then?'

The little ghost didn't answer. Mark saw his cobwebby hair spike out like Sam's fur. His big eyes almost popped out of his head.

'What is it? What can you see?' Mark stared around, but everything seemed ordinary in a high-up way.

'One two three four,' Grey whispered, and began to rise off the slates. 'One two three four.' He drifted sideways, leaving the rooftop.

'Wait for me!' Mark shouted, suddenly afraid. Without thinking he put out his arms . . . and found himself slithering down the slates. 'HELP!' He saw Cherry's scared face staring up from the path below just before he pitched into space.

He was falling, falling . . .

A tremendous jerk! The ground waiting to hit him, slid away beneath his nose. Now he was flying! Swooping up. Skimming the fence and the apple tree in Cherry's garden. Rising higher still over the roof of the bungalow shed, then sinking down, down, to land with a bump on the bungalow grass.

Grey pushed his fingers through his wild hair and blew out his cheeks. 'Wraiths and Shapes, that was a near shave!'

For a moment they looked at each other.

'You saved me,' Mark said shakily. 'How?'

'Grabbed you. Scruff of the neck. Seat of your breeches. That's how!' A big grin stretched Grey's bony face. 'Thank you.'

'What for?' Mark asked, amazed.

'Finding my chimney-pots for me.' Grey unfolded his bones and slid to the flowerpots that towered over the garden gnomes.

'That's two things you've found now,' Mark said. 'No, five — one rocking-horse and four chimney-pots.' Ticking them off on his fingers. 'All those things! We're really getting started now, aren't we? What's left?'

'A golden key. A green door. Six stone steps.' Grey stroked the chimney-pots. 'I think I can remember these standing on the roof . . . somewhere.'

'Like we did.' Mark forgot how scared he had been. 'It was great!'

'Like we will again, then!' Grabbing hold of Mark and puffing out his nightshift, Grey rose with him into the air. Together they whisked away. Bouncing down on the roof-top slates, then up again. Skimming a bus as they flew across the road. Sailing out to the pony drinking from its pond. Curving round and back across roof-tops to land on the path just as Cherry and Mum hurried out of the back door.

Mum slowed down. 'Cherry said you'd been on the roof! What's all this about falling?'

Mark looked at Grey, then at Cherry, then back at Mum. 'We were learning to fly,' he said. 'Grey was teaching me and I slipped. But he saved me so I didn't crash.' He could see she didn't believe one word.

'You and your silly games,' she said sharply. Then relented. 'No more frights please. Come in the kitchen. There is orange juice waiting for you both.'

'And for Grey,' Mark insisted.

'All right – Grey too!' Mum used the voice that meant she was playing along with his make-believe.

'I only like rainbow sandwiches and mist-shakes,' Grey reminded Mark. 'Sometimes a lick of barley-sugar twist.' But he followed them inside all the same.

4
A Key for Dressing Up

'Washday!' Dad said, putting Mark's clean clothes on the bottom of his bed. 'Hurry up and get dressed. We're going to the launderette after breakfast, with Gran.'

'Great . . . my MICE ARE NICE shirt!' Mark picked up a bright green Tee-shirt with brown letters and a yellow mouse on the front. He put it on.

Grey was perched on the rocking-horse, watching. He sighed gloomily.

'What's the matter?' Mark was pulling on stripy socks and clean jeans.

'Nothing,' Dad answered, rather surprised. 'Why?'

'Not you. Grey. He keeps going like this.'

Mark breathed in and out making a wheezing noise.

'Got a pain from eating too many sweets I shouldn't wonder!' Dad winked. He thought Grey was just another of Mark's pretend friends, but went along with it. Picking up the yesterday clothes, he took them downstairs.

When he had gone, Mark said: 'Have you?'

'What?' Grey rocked backwards and forwards.

'A pain.'

'No. Thinking, that's all.' Grey looked down at his tattered nightshirt and sighed again.

Mark stuffed his feet into his rabbit slippers. He was very hungry. Only a little bit of him was bothering with Grey. The rest was imagining cornflakes and buttered toast on the kitchen table.

'Aren't you going to come and have breakfast?' He couldn't wait to bite that toast!

Grey rocked harder. 'I told you before, ghosts only eat rainbows and misty things . . . and barley-sugar twists. There aren't any in your fridge. I've looked. I'll stay here.'

'Okay,' Mark said. 'Shan't be long.' He slid down the bannisters.

Grey heard him pad into the kitchen, and wondered what a Launderette was? He hoped it wouldn't be fierce. It must be important whatever it was, if you had to wear clean clothes to go and see it. His own clothes were a disgrace – dirty and full of holes. If only he had something smart to wear.

Creak creak creak, went the rocking-horse as if it was trying to tell him something. Creak creak creak.

'That's IT!' Grey said, and dived head first into the chest of drawers.

He came out with Mark's football jersey in his skinny hand.

'I'll look a regular bobby dazzler in this, don't you think?'

The rocking-horse said nothing.

Taking off his nightshirt, Grey began to struggle into the jersey. But the arms were too short and the neck hole was too small. Only wisps of cobwebby hair got to the other side.

He dropped the jersey on the floor and tried Mark's jacket. It was padded and green with a zip. He pulled at the zip. And pulled. AND PULLED . . .

His bones began to grumble: 'Tight tight tight tight . . .'

So that was no good either.

Grey scrowled at his nightshirt. He wasn't going to put on that old rag again. But without it he felt shivery and more see-through than ever. He looked around but couldn't see anything else in here. Gliding through the wall into the next room, he saw a wardrobe straight away.

He slid in.

Dresses and skirts, blouses and trousers, suits and shirts, hung neatly on a rail.

Grey's hair began to crackle. A ghost could feel proud of himself dressed in fancy clothes like these, he thought. How important he'd look! A real smart spook, brave enough to face the fiercest Launderette.'

He tried on a shiny blue dress with a large bow. But the top fell off his narrow shoulders. So he swapped it for a red skirt with white spots. On top of that he put on a hairy sports jacket. The skirt was long and nearly legged him over when he slipped from the wardrobe and went to the wall mirror. Even hovering above the carpet didn't help. It flapped and dragged round his feet. He was just bunching it out of the way when Mark came upstairs to fetch his shoes.

'Hey!' Mark made a dash at Grey. 'That's my mum's!' He grabbed the skirt. 'And that's my dad's!' Tugging at the jacket.

Grey hung on to both. 'What's all the fuss about?'

'They aren't yours. Take them off.' Mark tugged harder. Then suddenly let go. He stared at the mirror. 'Where are you?' He was looking at a skirt and jacket hanging by themselves in the air.

'Inside the clothes of course,' Grey said sulkily. 'Ghosts don't show up in mirrors.' He twirled round and the skirt flared out. 'Don't you think I look a bobby dazzler? I've been nothing but rags and tatters for so long. I do like a bit of colour.'

The clothes seemed to fade as Grey wore them. Mark thought they looked funny, but didn't like to say so.

'I know,' he said. 'If you put them back in the wardrobe, I'll find you something much better. Something you can keep.'

Grey didn't want to lose his beautiful clothes. 'What sort of something?'

'Wait and see.' Mark moved towards the door. 'Mum's gone to fetch the car, so get a move on or it'll be too late.'

Grey got a move on. He didn't want to miss the Something Better. He slid in and out of the wardrobe without bothering to open the door, and shivered after Mark into the kitchen.

Four big plastic bags leaned against the table. Three were blue. One was green. Mark dug into the green bag.

'This is for the jumble.' He threw out scarves, jumpers, knickers, saucepans, books, coats, stockings. 'Choose what you like.'

Grey hung back. What was this Jumble? Was it bigger than him? Did it have sharp teeth? Perhaps it wouldn't like ghosts! 'Won't the Jumble mind me taking things?' his teeth chattered.

'It's Gran's jumble. She won't mind.'

Grey felt better at once. He knew Gran. If the Jumble was her pet, like Plum, it must be all right. Plum was a friend. He fetched sticks when Grey blew them for him.

To be on the safe side, Grey checked on the Launderette's blue bags before deciding. They were full of smelly socks and grubby shirts and dirty towels. The Jumble's things were much nicer. He picked a boiler suit, a pink cardigan, a rainbow shawl – and put them on. There was a cheerful red bobble cap he fancied. He was about to put that on as well, when he spotted the hat. Not any old hat. This was the most wonderful hat he had seen in all his nights. Yellow straw. Swirls of gauzy net. Floppy red flower in front. Three tall feathers at the side. Silver ribbons tumbling down the back.

He put out his hand to take it.

Mark shook his head. 'That's Gran's party hat.'

'What's that about my hat?' Gran asked, coming into the kitchen and seeing her hat mistily through Grey. 'Has somebody left the kettle boiling? The kitchen's very steamy.'

Mark started to explain: 'It's not steam, it's . . .'

'What's all this mess?' Dad interrupted. He frowned at the heap of clothes on the floor.

Outside, the car horn tooted impatiently.

'Grey and me were only looking for something he could wear.' Mark began hurriedly stuffing everything back in the bag.

Dad helped because Mum was waiting. So did Grey. He and Dad got tangled together, arms reaching through each other like bits of weaving. Grey was so upset he got the hiccups, but Dad didn't notice.

At last they were all in the car. Mum driving, Dad beside her. Gran and Mark behind. Grey (wearing the party hat which he'd managed to grab at the last minute), was squashed with Plum in the luggage space.

'Here we are!' Mum said at last, stopping the car.

Everyone got out.

To Grey the place looked like an ordinary shop, with a window and a door. A pet shop, he wondered? Would there be a Launderette inside . . . perhaps a Jumble as well? He looked in and saw lots of metal boxes with little round windows. Water and bubbles sloshed about behind the glass. People were there too, pushing clothes into the boxes. Others were reading their newspapers. Cherry was there with her Mum.

'Where is it?' Grey asked Mark, who was lugging one of the blue bags.

'What?'

'The Launderette.'

'This is it, silly!' Mark went in. 'And these are the washing machines.'

It had never occurred to Grey that the Launderette was a *place*. What a good thing he'd decided to become a day-ghost. He was learning new things all the time.

Mark and Gran were loading a washing machine with dirty clothes, and Grey wanted to learn about this too. He went to help.

'That was quick!' Gran shut the little round window. She didn't see Grey standing there with her hat on.

Mark and Grey grinned at each other. They gave the machine some powder to eat.

'Swoosh!' said the machine. 'Glunk glunk glunk buzzzz . . .'

Grey stared as water poured down the inside of the window. Bubbles slapped and bounced. The clothes were having a roundabout ride.

'Hello!' said Cherry.

Grey didn't answer. Ghost-pimples covered his arms and legs as he watched the machine click and whir and begin to spin fast.

'Your hair's crackling,' Cherry said.

Under the hat, Grey's cobwebby hair was sending out little snapping flashes.

'You're on fire!' Mark said. 'Your hair's smoking!'

Spirals of pale smoke drifted from under the brim of Gran's hat. There was a smell of singeing.

Grey sniffed. 'You're right. It *is* me. I haven't felt this excited for years. It always happens when something tremendously exciting happens.'

People in the launderette were beginning to look worried. They sniffed, peered behind the machines and talked about smells of hot rubber.

Grey was beginning to feel very warm. He knew he should stop peeking at the thrilling roundabout inside the washing machine window, but the temptation was too strong.

'How will you put yourself out?' Mark whispered urgently. Smoke was coming from Grey's ears now.

'Like this!' Grey dived through the washing machine window.

'Stop it, stop it!' Mark dashed to the machine and tried to open it.

Then Gran and Mum and Dad made a dash at Mark, and everyone started talking at once. Including the launderette owner, who wanted to know what was going on?

Cherry did her best to explain. 'He went in because he was on fire and there's water in the machine to put him out.'

'What are you talking about, child?' Cherry's Mum had left her machine to join the little crowd.

'Grey, Mum. I'm talking about Grey.'

'And who is this Grey when he's at home?'

'The ghost who lives with Mark.'

Her Mum's eyebrows shot up like a lift and almost vanished under her hair. 'This isn't the time for making up stories,' she said.

'It's not a story,' Mark said. 'Grey *is* a ghost and he's in there now.' Pointing at the machine. 'And he went in head first in Gran's hat because he started burning. Ghosts do when they get very excited. Grey told us, didn't he Cherry?'

Cherry nodded.

'He doesn't need to break the glass to get

in I see,' Dad joked.

'He doesn't have to,' Mark told him.

Just then the machine washing Gran's clothes decided it had worked long enough. With a final CHUNK CLICK, it stopped. The clothes fell in a gentle heap at the bottom. There was no sign of Grey.

Cherry's Mum shook her head and went back to her own machine, muttering about 'Heads stuffed full of nonsense!'

Gran and Mum were pulling out pink stockings, pink vests, pink sheets, pink handkerchiefs, pink wiping-up towels. But there was still no ghost – pink or grey.

'Now however did that get in there?' Gran dragged out the soggy remains of her hat. 'It's red from that wretched flower that's done the mischief. I'm sure I put the hat out for the jumble sale. Not into the laundry bag.'

'Jumble SALE did you say?' Grey popped out of the back of the washing machine, face and hands smeary with oil. Sunshine from the launderette window passed through him making oily rainbow colours on the floor tiles. Grey didn't notice them. Nor did Gran. They were both staring at a thickened pinkish triangle of wool – all that was left of the rainbow shawl. Something glinted in one corner.

'My Golden Key!' Grey's hair crackled.

Gran seemed just as excited. 'Well I never, my brooch! All these years it's been lost.'

'Since you were a girl,' Grey reminded her.

'Since I was a girl,' Gran said, not hearing him.

'And all along I've been thinking I had to look for a golden key to fit my Green Door,' Grey said.

Mark felt confused. 'What are you talking about?'

'My brooch, dear,' Gran explained. 'It was in the shape of a key – a shining golden key! My Auntie Rose – that's your great-auntie – gave it to me for my seventh birthday.' Gran smiled, delighted to have it back. 'She gave me a shawl as well, for dressing up. How smart I used to think I was when I put it on.'

'And me,' Grey said.

Mark looked from one to the other. Gran was shaking her head and smiling as Mum and Dad examined the key. He moved close to Grey, whispering:

'Are you remembering now? Where were you when you first saw the key?'

Grey looked puzzled. 'I don't know.'

'But you *must*!'

'Well, I don't. I remember a bit here and a bit there, but not everything. That's the trouble.'

'Your brains need a polish.' Mark forgot to whisper and Gran caught the last word.

'Polish?' She rubbed at the key with her finger. 'You can clean it when we get home if you like.'

Mark was about to say 'Grey's brains, not the key' but gave up. He couldn't handle this three-way conversation, and decided to wait until he and Grey were on their own to try and sort things out properly.

It was a long wait.

Gran was so happy to have her brooch back, she took everyone to a café to celebrate. She treated them to coffee and ice-creams.

'Can I have two strawberry cones?' Mark asked.

Dad looked at him. 'Isn't that rather greedy?'

'No,' Mark said. 'One is for me and one is

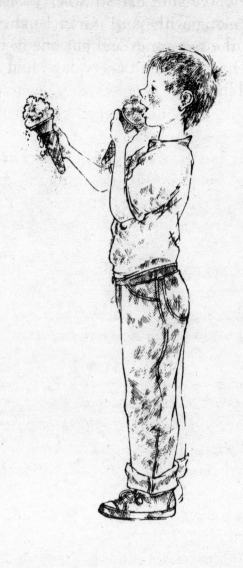

for Grey. We both like strawberry best.'

'Get along with you!' Gran laughed. She bought the two cones and put one in each of Mark's hands. 'It isn't every day I find a bit of my childhood.'

5
The
Green Door

'I've got to go to school today,' Mark said.

He was sitting at the breakfast table eating a marmalade sandwich. Grey was messing about with a crumb, trying to flick it into an empty teacup.

'What's school?' Grey asked.

'It's that place down the road with the climbing frame in the playground.' Mark added: 'Where we learn things.'

'Can I come with you?' Grey was anxious to learn things for himself. He had already learned a lot since becoming a day-ghost. All about launderettes and jumble sales and how to make an apple pie. Watching Mum rolling pastry, he had rolled it himself when her back was turned. He'd given the apples a stir in the saucepan and knew about adding sugar and cinnamon. But he didn't think apple pie tasted very nice. Give him a rainbow sandwich any day!

'But where would you sit?' Mark objected. 'There aren't any spare chairs in our classroom.'

'On the window-sill?' Grey suggested.

'Mrs Wilkins keeps our plants there, and the tadpoles.'

'I can stand up. I'll move about if you like.' Grey was willing to do anything. He was so keen to go.

Mark looked doubtful. He wasn't sure if Mrs Wilkins would like a ghost in her class, even if she couldn't see him.

'*Please*,' Grey begged.

'Oh all right.' Mark went to fetch his lunch-box and put on his anorak.

Grey couldn't wait to get there – but before they reached the school gates he began to feel less sure. The playground was so full. And what a din! Children were rushing about all over the place.

'Come on! There's Cherry and Darren . . .

and Winston and Lin and . . .' Mark was already running to join his friends.

Grey didn't hear the rest of their names. Suddenly shy, he drifted through the railings, hid behind a big dustbin and took a quick look round the side.

They were talking about pets.

The boy Mark called Darren, said: 'Winston's got a new gerbil.'

'And me!' Cherry chipped in. 'And I've got a hamster.' She nudged the girl next to her. 'Have you got pets, Lin?'

'Two guinea-pigs.' Lin blew out a bubble of gum and burst it. 'My sister had a puppy for her birthday.'

'I've got six puppies,' said a boy with hair like broom bristles.

Lin blew and burst another gum bubble. 'You're a liar, Stuart Timmins.'

'Not!' said Stuart fiercely.

'Are!'

'Not!'

'Oh shut up! Puppies aren't that special,' Cherry said. She turned to Mark. 'Go on, tell them about your pet. You know – your ghost.'

'Grey isn't a pet.' Mark glanced round,

trying to find him. 'He's my friend.'

Behind the dustbin, Grey went pink with pleasure. But Stuart let out a snort of laughter. 'Now who's a liar! A *ghost?*' He began to hop up and down, chanting: 'Mark's got a gho-ost, Mark's got a toastie ghostie!'

Mark went bright red and rushed at him. They flopped on the ground in a heap, rolling over and over.

Somebody shouted: 'FIGHT!' and as Grey slid through the dustbin in alarm, Lin caught sight of him. He was wondering if he ought to try and blow them apart, when a large woman in a long red skirt and black jersey, hurried across the playground.

Lin kept staring at Grey. 'Miss!' she squeaked. 'Miss, there's a ghost.'

Winston spun round. His eyes grew enormous. 'Look, Miss – by the dustbin!'

Mrs Wilkins pushed through the excited crowd, grabbed the two struggling boys by their shoulders, and with a shake, stood them on their feet. 'Any more of that,' she said sharply, 'and you won't be going to see our models and paintings in the museum this morning.'

Grey pricked up his pointed ears. Museum? Models and paintings?

'Are we going in the minibus?' Stuart asked eagerly.

'And can Grey come too?' Cherry added.

'Grey?' Mrs Wilkins still had Mark and Stuart by the shoulders.

'Mark's ghost,' Cherry said before Mark could shake his head to stop her. 'He's there by the dustbin.'

Mrs Wilkins raised her eyebrows. 'You've all been watching too much telly by the sound of it! Now get into line. The bell will go any minute.'

She had hardly finished speaking when the bell clanged. Grey drifted to the railings, watching the children troop into school. Some of them turned and waved, but he was still feeling too shy to go with them. When the door was shut and everything quiet, he slid in through the school wall.

On the other side was a place full of coats and anoraks and wash-basins. A good place to wait until it was museum time, he decided. Turning on several taps, he splashed about happily. By the time the children came back to collect their outdoor clothes, he had managed to make a lot of puddles on the floor, and a rainbow of spots on the window.

'Who left those taps running?' Mrs Wilkins asked crossly as she turned them off.

Grey slid hastily outside again.

The minibus was parked by the school gates. He wandered around it, sliding in and out until the children arrived, whisking out of the way while they climbed in. When everyone was settled, he looked through the windscreen to see where Mark was sitting. But the driver was in the way. Grey leaned closer. Next thing he knew, a jet of soapy water squirted straight through his head and hung on his bones. Something hit him on the nose. As he jumped back, there was Mark inside, doubled up laughing!

Grey shook himself like a wet grumpy dog. Water flicked off his bones, and he heard the minibus start up.

'Wait for me!' he shouted, but the driver didn't hear. The minibus moved out into the street, gathering speed, and Grey shot after it, gulping in air and pumping it out. Flying with the birds over the stream of traffic. Everything was flowing towards the middle of town.

How he hated towns!

Now and again a few birds stopped off to perch on trees and window-sills, but Grey flew steadily. Below him were little lorries and cars and vans and bikes and bigger buses and tiny people on foot – even a small man riding a miniature horse, but . . .

No minibus, Grey thought suddenly. Holy spooks! He swooped under a railway bridge, hunting for it. Then over the top, getting mixed up with a train.

The train whistle shrieked.

Hair stiff with fright, bones rattling, Grey spun away, going round a tall chimney, round a church spire, round a block of towering flats.

Still no minibus.

At last, dizzy and almost ready to turn tail and bolt, he spotted a familiar blue speck in a car park. The car park was at the back of a big building. Minibus and museum together!

Grey was so relieved he tumbled straight through the roof-slates, through the room-space below, through the floor under that, down, down to land in the middle of a miniature village. He was very glad to be

there. Anywhere was better than town.

'Hey!' Mark said. 'You're sitting on my house. Where have you been?'

There was a rope around the village. Mark was on the other side of the rope. Grey looked at him dizzily. On the other side of Mark was a wall with a window. On the other side of the window was a street full of traffic. Town after all?

'Grey!' Cherry leaned over the rope, trying to take his hand. 'We were worried. We thought you'd got lost.'

Grey held her hand tight. 'I thought I'd lost all of *you*.' He began to feel better.

Mark was tugging at Cherry's arm. 'Get off! You're squashing my house. Let go of her, Grey!'

Letting go, Grey looked down at the village.

69

There were trees and cottages. Fields with cows and sheep. A farmyard with a cart and horse. Barns. A dog. Two cats. Several miniature hens. The farm was there too, and something else.

Through Dad's old gardening trousers and his own knobbly knees, Grey saw a house that was larger than the other village buildings. Tall plasticine chimneys sat on top of a pointed painted cardboard roof. Windows and front door were pointed and painted as well. Plants were painted as if they grew up the walls of the houses. It didn't look at all like the home-place where Mark lived. Grey was puzzled.

'*Your* house?'

Mark explained. 'Not where I live. This house is a bit of our town in the old days. We've been learning about it at school. How it used to be.'

'When it was a village,' Cherry added. 'Our class has done a long painting of the village street. See – on that wall?'

Grey got off Mark's house and drifted through the rope for a closer look. He felt shivery and excited, as if something special was waiting for him round a corner. A few sparks crackled in his cobwebby hair. He took no notice of the other children, but they noticed him. Gradually, in ones and twos, then in little groups, they moved towards him.

'I painted that house and those trees,' Mark said.

'And I did the girl with the hoop, and the milkcart.' Cherry pointed them out.

'The little cottage?' Grey felt he almost knew that cottage, but something wasn't quite right. 'Who painted that?' He heard a small gulp of breath.

'Me,' Lin squeaked. 'You talk!' She touched him and squeaked again as her fingers went into his hand.

Stuart gave a harder poke, wriggling his fingers inside Grey's arm. 'He's cold.'

'And you're hot. Get off!' Grey twitched.

The children began whispering to each other: 'He talks. . . .' 'That ghost can talk like us. . . .' 'He must be real. . . .' 'No he isn't, you can see through him. . . .' 'Scary. . . .' 'No he isn't. . . .' 'Ghosts aren't supposed to talk. . . .'

'We can if we want to,' Grey said. 'And I am real. I'm a real spook.' To prove it, he slid through the painting. There was nothing behind except the wall. He slid through that, then back again, stopping to poke his head through Lin's cottage window.

By now all the class was grouped round the painting, pointing at Grey and giggling. Left alone, Mrs Wilkins looked to see where they were. She came to join them.

'I'm not surprised you want to keep looking at your painting.' She smiled, but not at Grey. 'It's one of the best things here. Different from our model village, but just as good.'

Grey agreed. Poking his hands through the cottage wall, he clapped.

Mrs Wilkins took no notice. 'Come over here a minute all of you. I've found something rather interesting.' She led the reluctant class back to the glass case.

Grey went too.

There were several old things inside the case. A book made from horn, with a handle. Two school slates with their pencils, Goose feather pens. But Grey saw only the picture – a painting of an old house, half hidden by

trees. Pointed roof-tops rose above the trees.
A field stretched in front with a curling road.
At the bottom was a cottage, very like Lin's,
with lace curtains at the windows and a smoking chimney. But the front door was different.

Grey knew this door was right. 'My door!
Look, Mark, that's my *Green Door!*' A big
grin stretched out his thin face. He began to
dance about. 'It's my old home-place. 'If only
I knew where it is.'

'That's the cottage I painted,' Lin said. 'But
I gave mine a blue door.'

Mrs Wilkinson nodded. 'Thought you'd
find it interesting. A hundred years ago a girl
lived in that house. She painted this picture.'

Grey's hair was sparking. 'It's my home-place,' he repeated.

'You lived in my cottage?' Lin was amazed.

'Not me – *she!*' Mrs Wilkins laughed, not
understanding. 'And not in the cottage.
You're getting in a muddle. *She* lived in the
big house.'

Grey pointed at himself. 'I haunted all of it.
The big house. The field. Those trees. The
cottage. Everywhere . . . but this is only a
picture! He knew about pictures now. They

were flat with nothing to see on the other side. He sighed. 'And don't bother trying to explain about me. She's grown-up. She doesn't know I'm here.'

'Never mind,' Cherry whispered. 'The rest of us can see you, can't we, Lin?'

'Yes – and hear you.'

They both wanted to hold his hands and he let them. Then everyone wanted a turn, and in the minibus going back to school they all wanted to sit by him.

'Never knew such a fidgety lot!' Mrs Wilkins said as they took turns sitting inside Grey's knobbly knees, or touching his pointed ears, or putting their fingers into his hands, or trying to plait his flyaway hair.

'You will come to school again, won't you?' Lin whispered as they got off the minibus by the school gates.

'I might,' he said.

'I like your friends,' Grey told Mark that night. He was sitting on the rocking-horse. Mark was in bed. 'And I like being here.'

'Do you?' Mark sat up. 'Really?'

'Yes, really – but I wish I knew where to find the home-place. Do you know?'

Mark made a hill with his knees and leaned his elbows on it. 'I think the house isn't there now. I think it might have got knocked down.'

'Knocked down?' Grey's face grew long and green. *Knocked down?* But why? Whatever shall I do?'

'I don't know why, but you can stay here with me.' Mark looked at him anxiously. 'You will stay won't you? You can stay forever and ever.'

Grey was still muttering: 'Knocked down knocked down . . .' hunched up on the horse.

'I'm so glad you didn't get lost,' Mark added.

Grey seemed to come to himself. He uncurled and shook out his bones. 'No need to worry – my bones wouldn't let me stray too far from home.'

'This is home?' Mark asked eagerly.

Grey looked all the way round the room until he got back to Mark. He patted the neck of the rocking-horse and stroked its mane. 'Y'know,' he said slowly, 'I really think it is.'

'But what about that house and the cottage?'

'A picture,' Grey said, a little sadly. 'Nobody can live in a picture. No spook can *haunt* a picture. Anyway, a proper home-place needs people.'

Mark yawned and lay back on his pillow. 'I'm people.'

'I know.'

Mark closed his eyes contentedly. Then opened them again. 'What about the six stone steps? They weren't in the picture, or in our model.'

'I know that too.'

'We'll have to find them. I'll help you. We'll look tomorrow, or the next day, or . . . the . . . next. . . .' He breathed deeply.

'Goodnight!' Grey said, and slipping off the horse, posted himself into his chest-of-drawer bed.

6
A Game of Cricket

It was very hot. For days and days the summer sun had been shining. When Mark woke up there was another blue sky outside his bedroom window. Sparrows chattered in the apple tree. Dust danced in a sunbeam.

He leapt out of bed, remembering. 'Holidays! Grey, where are you? It's the holidays!'

Grey came out of the drawer where he had been asleep on Mark's socks. He stretched, and his cobwebby hair crackled.

'Does that mean no school?' he asked, yawning.

'No school for weeks and weeks!' Mark was scrambling into shorts and his MICE ARE NICE shirt. 'Come on! There's lots to do.'

Grey felt disappointed. He liked school and had been planning to make a plasticine ghost. Taking off his nightshirt, he put on his favourite pink cardigan and a pair of Dad's old gardening trousers.

'Lots of what?' he asked, trailing downstairs after Mark.

'Oh . . . things.' Mark was trying to decide whether to have cornflakes or a boiled egg. He sat down at the kitchen table and ate some toast to help himself think.

There were no rainbow sandwiches for Grey's breakfast. Nor any mist-shake. Not even a barley-sugar twist. In fact there was nothing for him at all. He wandered about and got walked through by Mum on her way to the sink. It was all rather upsetting. After-wards he followed Mark into the garden.

Cherry was sitting on the fence with Sam. She called to them:

'Look what my dad's given me!'

Leaning over her side of the fence, she pulled up a long piece of polished wood. It had a handle at the top.

'What's that?' Grey asked.

'Cricket bat, silly!' Mark said.

'Don't you know about cricket, Grey?' Cherry asked, as if nobody could be that stupid.

'All right . . . all right,' Grey said in a huff. 'The only sort of cricket I know, hops about.' He glided to the fence. 'Show me what you do with this bat.'

'Not here,' Cherry said. 'Not enough space.'

'We could play at the park,' Mark suggested. 'I'll bring my cricket ball.'

'I've got some stumps.' Cherry slid down and ran off to get them.

Grey wished he had something for the cricket. All he could think of was his pink cardigan. He worried about this as they walked along the same friendly road that had first brought him to Mark's house. Today the road wandered between houses and shops until it reached a wooden gate. Behind was a path leading to a big patch of grass backed by a tall hedge. They went in.

'This'll do.' Cherry had been carrying three round sticks of wood. She pushed them side by side into the grass. 'Stumps,' she told Grey. 'And bails.' Balancing another stick on top.

'But there's only enough for one end.'

'End of what?' Grey asked.

'The wicket,' Mark said. 'The batsman has to run up and down the wicket.' He was looking round for something else to use as stumps, and pointed to the top of a nearby tree. 'That broken branch would do. Only it's too high up.'

'I'll get it!' Grey said eagerly. Glad of this chance to do his bit for the cricket. Puffing out his chest, he floated to the tree-top, grabbed the branch and came down like a lift. 'Stumps!' he said proudly, offering it to Mark.

Mark strode away, counting: 'One two three four . . .' At twenty he stuck the branch in the ground.

'Now what?' Grey asked as he came back.

'The bowler runs up and throws the ball,' Cherry told him.

'And the batsman hits it then runs,' Mark said.

'If she can. If she hits the ball hard enough.'

'Or he isn't caught out by the fielder . . .'

'Or she isn't run out . . .'

'Or he might be LBW . . .'

'Or . . .'

'Hold your HORSES!' Grey was in a proper muddle. 'All these he's and she's! How do you expect an ordinary sort of spook to make sense of it all?'

'We'll play, then you'll get the idea.' Mark took a penny from the pocket of his shorts. 'Toss to see who bats first. Heads it's you, Cherry. Tails it's me.'

'Hold your horses,' Grey said again. He didn't mean to be left out. 'What do I have to do?' He rolled up his pink sleeves.

'You be fielder. Stand there!' Mark pointed to a spot between stumps and hedge. 'When a ball comes, catch it.'

'Won't it go straight through him?' Cherry asked.

'A ball is a thing,' Mark told her. 'Grey can hang on to things.'

Cherry wasn't convinced. 'What about doors and walls then? I've seen him go through those. That means they go through him. Like the ball will.'

Grey began to feel as if he wasn't there. He leaned forward and waved. 'Hello there! Remember me?'

'That's better,' he smoothed down his hair.

'If you must know *I* decide about these things. If I want to go through a wall, I do. If I want to hang on to a ball, I can. All part of a ghost's stock in trade. Animals are different. They always go through me.'

'Not always,' Mark argued, siding with Cherry. 'I'm a sort of animal and you hang on to me sometimes. Remember how you tried to pull me through the fence?'

'You got stuck,' Grey said.

'I know – but you held my hand tight all the time.'

'Yes . . . well . . .' Grey couldn't quite

understand this either. He began talking about something else quickly. 'Toss your groat and let's get started.'

'My groat?' Mark looked at the penny in his hand.

'Penny, I mean.' Grey felt flustered. Money had changed so much since he was a ghostling. Groats and guineas then. Now it was pounds and pence. He mopped his face with his cardigan sleeve and slid to his fielding spot.

Mark tossed.

Cherry won.

Grey watched Mark walk away down the wicket, past the tree-branch-stumps, without stopping. Was he going home, Grey wondered? But Mark turned and began to run back fast. As he reached the stumps he hurled the ball as hard as he could. It bounced. Shot past Cherry's outstretched bat. Went through Grey's pink cardigan middle . . . and buried itself in the hedge.

'Owk!' Grey shook out his crumpled bones.

'You were supposed to catch that!' Mark shouted.

Grey stalked grumpily to the hedge. 'Bossy!' he muttered. 'Not my fault. How do I know what to do?' He pulled out the ball. 'Stand there! Catch that! What does he think I am . . . a machine?' He was tossing the ball from hand to hand, so busy grumbling he didn't see the woman stop and watch. She gaped at the ball hopping about by itself in mid-air. Her dog saw it too.

With a loud bark, the dog sprang. Snapping.

'Get off!' Grey saw the sharp teeth and imagined the ball gobbled up. No ball, no cricket!

He did the only thing he could think of –

hurling it high, he took a deep breath and *BLEEEW!* Away went the ball, climbing into the sky until it was no more than a speck.

Caught in the middle of a leap, the dog spung like a top as the ghost-breath hit him. Up, up he went . . . and down, down. Landing with a thump he took off with rocket speed, yelping.

'Blot . . . Blot!' the woman shouted, looking back over her shoulder as if she couldn't believe what had happened. 'You mutton-headed clot of a dog! BLOT!'

Cherry and Mark began to giggle. They watched Grey back towards the hedge, hands outstretched. Saw the ball grow larger, Larger, LARGER . . . and disappear on the wrong side of the hedge.

There was a splintering crash of glass breaking.

They started to run towards the hedge as Grey helicoptered into the air until he could see over the top.

'*Holy spooks!*' his hair shot sparks.

'What's happened?'

'Can you see?'

'Is it a window?'

'GREY!' Mark bellowed. 'What is it?'

Grey glanced back briefly as he skimmed the hedge-top. 'Six stone steps, that's what. *Six stone steps!*' and he sank out of sight.

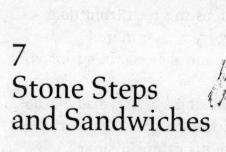

7
Stone Steps
and Sandwiches

There was a small gap in the park hedge. Mark peered through and saw a garden with a greenhouse. The cricket ball had smashed a pane of glass and lay on the floor inside. Beyond the greenhouse was a flight of old steps. Stone steps. They led up to the front door of a cottage. He knew that green front door and the old cottage straightaway. They were the same as the door and cottage in the picture.

Grey was there. Sitting on the top step, hugging his knobbly knees and singing to himself. Mark knew the tune – 'Twinkle twinkle little star' – but the words were different. Grey-words.

'Rocking-horse and green front door
Chimney-pots one two three four
Golden Key that shines so bright
Like a sunbeam in the night
Six stone steps to green front door
Now I've got you evermore.'

Sparks crackled and danced round his cobwebby hair.

'His ears are smoking.' Cherry had her nose
pushed right into the hedge. 'We'd better get
there quick before his cardigan singes.'

'We'll go round,' Mark said. 'Come on!'

Together they ran out of the park, along the
road, through an open iron gate to the path
beyond, across grass and round the corner of
the cottage just as the front door began to
open.

'Grey!' Mark called.

'Mark!' Gran answered, amazed to see him
there. 'Was it your ball that broke my greenhouse?' She came out of the cottage on to the
top step.

Mark was just as amazed. 'Yes. But that
isn't your greenhouse.'

'It is now,' Gran said. 'I used to live here as
a girl. Now I've bought it back again from Mr

Cox. We were children together. That's right, isn't it?' She turned to an old man in a big jersey and carpet slippers, who stood on the top step.

He nodded. 'Quite right, Hilda. Is this your grandson?'

Mark was amazed all over again. He had forgotten his Gran was called Hilda.

'My father was gardener then,' Hilda-Gran went on, 'and this cottage belonged to the big house. "The Haunted House" people called it. But the house was pulled down when the new estate was built, and there's no ghost any more.'

'Yes there is,' Mark said. 'He came back. You're standing in him.'

Startled, Gran looked at her feet, then over her shoulder. 'What ghost?'

'Grey,' Mark said, staring at Grey who was staring at the old man. 'I'm talking about my friend, Grey.'

'Oh *that* ghost!' Gran said as if it was all a game of pretend.

Grey had a smile like a quarter-moon. He jumped up. Going to the old man he seized his hand. 'Blow me down, if it isn't Albert grown old. Remember me, Albert?' He began pumping Albert's hand up and down. 'What larks we had. Hide-and-seek around the chimney-pots. What tricks we played!'

Albert was gazing at his hand as it waggled in the air.

'He can't see you,' Cherry said.

'But we used to be such pals.' Grey lost his moon smile. 'Years ago. When we lived in the haunted house.'

'Years ago,' Cherry repeated. 'That's it! He was a boy then.'

'Boys can see you,' Mark said.

'And girls,' Cherry added.

'But not grown-up folk.' Grey shook his head and looked so upset Mark caught hold of his hand. Then he took Albert's spare hand, squeezing it.

'Grey's here, Albert. Can't you remember? Can't you *see*?'

They stood in a ring. Albert squeezed up his eyes, leaning forward and peering as if through a thick mist. Then he began to smile.

The smile grew.

'Well I'll go to the foot of our stairs!' he said at last. 'MY GHOST!' He almost shouted.

'And mine,' Mark said.

Albert slapped Grey's shoulder, then looked alarmed, feeling for Mark's hand again. 'For a minute then, I thought I'd lost you. Y'do come and go! Where have you been all these years?'

'Here and there,' Grey said. 'I'm living with Mark now. Didn't fancy the idea of haunting a new house at first, even though it is built on top of the old home-place. But my bones feel comfortable, and they are right. We have central heating, and I've got a most cosy bed.'

Albert laughed. 'You old softie!'

Gran looked from Albert to Mark to Cherry then back at Albert again. 'What's got into everyone? All of you talking at thin air. Have you gone silly?'

Cherry took her by the hand and broke the ring. Then mended it again by linking hands with Albert. 'You hold Mark's hand,' she told Gran. 'There. *Now* do you see?'

Gran's eyes widened. She saw the pink cardigan first of all. Then the old gardening trousers. Then wild hair. Then a long pale face with popping eyes. Long fingers. Long feet.

'Mark's Grey,' she said wonderingly.

Grey's quarter-moon smile came back. His pointed ears wriggled happily.

'And you're the old ghost from the haunted house?'

'Not that old,' Grey said quickly. 'But yes, they called the home-place haunted because I used to nip round corners and give folk a surprise now and again.'

'I saw you once,' Gran went on. 'Did you know that?'

It was Grey's turn to be surprised. 'No. Where?'

'I was sitting on my rocking-horse,' Gran said. 'It had a red saddle in those days and stood by the window in this cottage. My seventh birthday it was, and I had on the rainbow shawl and key brooch. You were outside, standing on your head on the grass.'

'Aaah!' Grey said softly, as if he understood a lot of things.

'Go on,' Mark begged. 'Is there some more? Tell us.'

Gran smiled. 'It's a long story.'

'We like long stories,' Cherry said.

'They go with tea and cake, don't you

think?' Albert suggested. He drew them into the cottage kitchen. 'We could have a picnic.'

Grey looked along the jampots standing in neat rows on the kitchen shelves. 'I don't suppose you have a spare rainbow about you?' he asked wistfully. 'I haven't had a rainbow sandwich in years.'

Albert shook his head. 'I'm right out of rainbows.' He took a tin from the end of a jam shelf and brought out a chocolate cake.

That was when Mark had his idea. He told Albert about it quietly.

They spread a rug on the grass for their picnic. Albert carried out a loaded tray. Mark carried one plate.

'What have we got?' Cherry asked.

Albert put the tray on the rug. 'Crisps, pork

pie, tomatoes, honey sandwiches, chocolate cake, bananas, lemonade, tea . . .'

'And a *rainbow* sandwich.' Mark put the plate in front of Grey.

For a moment, Grey stared at it. Then he turned the plate round and gazed at it from the other side. He took off the lid of bread. Inside were rainbow stripes of jam.

'Purple blackcurrant, blue bilberry, green gooseberry, yellow plum, orange marmalade, red cherry,' Mark said, watching him anxiously.

Grey prodded the jam with a skinny finger. Licked it. Prodded and licked again. Finally he took a bite.

'It isn't a real rainbow,' Mark said.

'I know that,' Grey said, spitting crumbs. 'But it tastes good.' He took another bite. 'Know what, Mark?'

'What?'

Grey's smile stretched from ear to ear. 'It tastes better than good. It tastes of home!'